Valentine
Mice!

Valentine Mice!

by Bethany Roberts

Illustrated by Doug Cushman

Green Light Readers
HOUGHTON MIFFLIN HARCOURT
Boston   New York

First Green Light Readers edition, 2016

www.hmhco.com

The Library of Congress has cataloged the hardcover edition as follows:

Roberts, Bethany.
Valentine mice!/by Bethany Roberts; illustrated by Doug Cushman.
p. cm.
Summary: An energetic group of mice deliver valentines to the other animals.
[1. Valentines—Fiction. 2. Mice—Fiction.] I. Cushman, Doug, ill. II. Title.
PZ7.R5396Val   1997
[E]—dc21   96-50889
                                                              CIP
                                                              AC

ISBN: 978-0-395-77518-9 hardcover
ISBN: 978-0-547-37144-3 board book
ISBN: 978-0-544-80898-0 GLR paperback
ISBN: 978-0-544-80897-3 GLR paper over board

Manufactured in China
SCP 10 9 8 7 6 5 4 3 2 1

4500615597

To my valentines, Bob,
Krista and Melissa —B.R.

To Juney Irene Cushman,
my first valentine
—D.C.

Valentine mice
deliver valentines—

red, pink.
Skip! Hop!

Up this hill,
then s-l-i-d-e down.

One little mouse
goes *swoosh!* Plop!

One to the rabbit,
two for the squirrels,

three for the chipmunks.
Zip! Nip!

More to deliver.

Cross the pond.

S-l-i-d-e!   G-l-i-d-e!

Slip!   Flip!

Valentines here!

Valentines there!

Shower valentines!

THROW! THROW! THROW!

Valentine mice—
one, two, three . . .

One is missing!
Where can he be?

Valentine mice
look high and low.

Hurry! Worry!
Call! Shout!

Follow these footprints.
Quick! Quick!

There's a mitten!

Pull him out!

All together now . . .

Dig!   Tug!

Push!   P-u-l-l!

YAY!

One little mouse gets a

valentine hug.